Dragons in Spring
Chapbook Anthology

Edited by B. Heather Mantler

Laughter

ISBN: 978-1-927507-54-4

TABLE OF CONTENTS

Order and Chaos
Jennie Evans

"There is an order to everything. You know this, Ra-el."

"Yes, sir," he bowed his head in respect. Flecks of dust floated past his downturned eyes, glinting in the late afternoon sunbeams from the cracked ceiling above. The floor, grey stone bricks, was cool against his scales. He raised his head and looked past Order Falsyn to the stained glass set into the wall. It was a piece he knew all too well; he lost count of the number of hours he had spent as a child tracing every line, memorizing every coloured pane.

"We cannot grace those below with our magic. While we may walk amongst them, we will never be them."

There were angels at the highest point, but the largest section of the stained glass depicted the Order of the Nephilim. Several winged serpents of varying colour, his kind, looked on with eyes shining in the sun. They stood above the common folk, daring not to look at them. Below that, the demonoids and the Chaos of Devils. It was a balanced structure.

"This is not your first infraction. You know better," Order Falsyn emphasized, his composure momentarily slipping. He inhaled deeply, rolling his shoulders back. He slithered over to a window, turning away from Ra-el.

They both stood in silence for longer than was comfortable, but Ra-el didn't dare leave. He thought back to the times he'd used his magic to help common folk. Most times were fairly harmless—healing broken ankles, repairing dropped vases, making flowers bloom—but the latest interaction was comparatively severe. A young woman had been mauled by wild animals and would have died from her wounds had he not used his magic to heal her. In doing so, he altered her fate. Messing around in the affairs of commoners was deeply frowned upon by the Order.

He'd been chided for his actions before, but something was different this time. Order Falsyn turned to face him. His expression was not one of disappointment or sadness; it was one of cold stoicism.

"The Order has discussed the matter and come to a conclusion. Your existence as a fellow member tarnishes all our reputations. As such, we have decided to revoke your status and powers that come from being in the Order. If you wish to grovel in the dirt with common folk, then so be it. You can join them."

Order Falsyn's words hit Ra-el like a sack of bricks. Despite the formality, simply put, it was a death sentence. The very essence of a Nephilim depended on their angelic powers, and without them, the person would grow ever sicker and weaker until they died.

"Please, sir, you can't... I, no..." Ra-el babbled, desperate to talk his way out.

"There's nothing you can do to change the decision. It is final."

Order Falsyn approached Ra-el slowly, hands behind his back. It would take him only a few seconds to take away Ra-el's powers.

Ra-el panicked. His eyes darted around the room frantically. He couldn't win against the man in a fight, not that he was keen on drawing his blade against a fellow member anyhow. None of the guards or others would help him either. His only option was to flee.

He spread his wings and flew straight for the door, flinging it open with force. He was quick to keep flying, Order Falsyn already in pursuit.

"You can't escape, Ra-el," Order Falsyn raised his voice.

Townsfolk stared at Ra-el in shock as he darted past them. As they realized what was happening, several of them took flight to pursue him.

"After him!" Order Falsyn ordered, and more Nephilim joined the pursuing mob.

Ra-el flapped his feathered wings quicker, gaining height to rise above the town. Once clear of it, he tucked his wings in and angled sharply downward to skim low over the plains. Flowers were starting to bloom after winter's thaw, shades of pink, yellow, and red dotting the lush green grasslands. It would have been beautiful were he not hurtling past it in a frenzy.

Ahead, the plains abruptly ended. With a last burst of speed, Ra-el shot over the edge of his floating island home and plunged headfirst into a freefall. He could see nothing but clouds coming to meet him at high speeds.

Order Falsyn landed just before the edge of the meadows. "Pursue him, and bring him back here to me," he commanded. Dozens of Nephilim hurtled past and dropped off the edge.

Ra-el couldn't see anything except white. Condensation formed on his scales and slid off just as quickly. It was hard to breathe, but he didn't slow his descent. He broke through the bottom of the clouds and saw the vast ocean below. As it rushed to meet him, he spread his wings and angled himself toward land. Endless trees covered the ground, but he was flying too fast to enter the canopy.

He chanced a glance behind him and spotted the other Nephilim hot on his trail. He wouldn't have time to hide, not yet. His muscles already burned from exertion, but his primal sense of self-conservation propelled him onward.

Mountains rose above the forests. Ra-el flew close to the rocky cliffs, looking for a way to lose his pursuers. He veered to the left and darted between two close rock faces, narrowly avoiding clipping his wings on the stone. Another sharp turn slipped him between jagged columns. He took the precious few seconds he had gained to drop down into the forest.

Here, he slowed his frantic flight. It wouldn't do him any good to fly at full speed into a tree, and the smaller branches were potentially dangerous too. He wove through tree trunks, heart pounding. The sun had nearly set, and thankfully, the darkness brought him some camouflage. If not for the encroaching night, his bright blue scales would have given him away in an instant.

He came to a clearing in the trees, and just beyond was a forest village. He yearned to enter the town and ask for refuge, but the logical part of his mind told him that was a bad idea. Common folk rarely ever saw the Nephilim, and if a group of half-angels asked them where Ra-el was hiding, they would no doubt give him away.

Beyond the village, however, another mountain loomed. Out of breath and with wings burning, Ra-el figured it was his last hope of finding a hiding place. The exposed limestone hinted at caves, and when he approached the rock, it didn't take him long to find one. The entrance was fairly spacious, but a clump of trees and bushes obscured most of it. He checked over his shoulder to see if anyone was watching him, but saw no Nephilim. He slipped into the cave.

As he slithered in farther, he suddenly froze dead in his tracks. As his eyes adjusted to the dimness of the cave, a large shape materialized from the rocky walls. It was easily double his length and more than twice as thick. Sharp, pointed scales ran in rows, disappearing into the inky darkness. The smell hit him shortly after. Mud, decay, and a metallic tinge to the air that overpowered everything else. Blood, fresh.

The beast shifted, sensing another presence in the grotto. A giant head swung around to face the intruder, more rows of spikes glinting in the moonlight. Dark red eyes glowered at Ra-el, narrow, suspicious.

"If you think you can just come here to finish me off, you'll sorely regret it," a deep voice boomed. The dragon struggled to rise. His back arched, his tail unfurled, and his wings unfolded. He was massive.

"I, uh, no no," Ra-el stuttered, flinching instinctively. "I'm not here to kill anyone. I'm looking for a place to hide." The dragon's head was inches away from Ra-el's own. Its scales were dark purple, he noticed in passing, and its acrid breath was the source of the stench of decay. The dragon was a demonoid, Ra-el was fairly certain of that.

The beast looked skeptical, and surveyed him further. "You're not from the village, then." It was more of a statement than a question. He paused for a second, then lowered his head and growled. "Get out."

That was the absolute last thing Ra-el wanted to do. By now, the other Nephilim would have caught up to his last known position. Going out would expose him and surely get him caught. This cave was his last hope and murderous dragon or not, he was staying. He rose up and steeled his gaze.

"You're hurt." He gestured to the slick blood on the beast's hide, now confident it was its own.

"What's your point?" the monster snapped, defensive.

"I'm just saying, if you want to lounge around until someone comes to kill you, fine. Or, let me hide out here and I'll heal your wounds. Your call." He was feeling bold, whether from the adrenaline or his nerves he couldn't tell.

The dragon hesitated, raised his snout, and sniffed at the air. This seemed to reassure him, and he relaxed back into a laying position. He nodded.

"Part angel, aren't you? Fine. But no funny business or else." He barred his dagger-like teeth.

Ra-el cautiously approached the wounded dragon. He had used his magic to heal many others before, but never anything this large or volatile. Now that he was closer, he could see the dragon's body rising and falling as he breathed. Every once in a while, his breathing would hitch from a twinge of pain, disrupting the mesmerizing motion.

He placed his hands against the dragon's hide near its shoulder and closed his eyes. He inhaled. In his mind, he called out to his ancestors and drew from their power. A blue glow enveloped his hands. He exhaled. Tendrils of blue curled out from his splayed fingers and washed over the dragon's body. In their wake they mended deep gashes. As the last tendrils fizzled out, Ra-el opened his eyes and sunk into a slouch, a wave of fatigue hitting him with dizzying speed.

"Okay, you should be alright now."

The dragon stared at Ra-el, then down at its own body. He unfurled one wing and flapped it up and down. He seemed satisfied with the result. Heaving himself upright, he circled around the cave and settled into a more comfortable position.

"Alright, guess you can stay."

Ra-el gave a tired smile and slithered farther into the cave, away from the nakedness of the entrance. He laid down against one of the walls, exhausted, but his mind was racing. Now that the adrenaline was wearing off, his thoughts swirled with the makings of guilt.

He had just healed a demonoid. If he wasn't even allowed to help common folk, then helping a demon was completely out of the question. And yet, here he was, and he had. He envisioned Order Falsyn staring at him disapprovingly, the rest of the Order behind him. Each and every one of their gazes was filled with anger, sadness, and disappointment. What he had done was wrong, but the guilt he felt was from letting down the Order, not from helping a creature of chaos. Maybe Order Falsyn is right. Maybe I don't deserve to be a Nephilim. He huffed in frustration.

He tried to push the thoughts to the side. It was late,

and he needed to rest in order to face whatever would come his way tomorrow. He focused on the ambient sounds around him. The breathing of the large dragon was the loudest, reverberating in the small space. Wind whistled past the cave's entrance, and beyond that, the faint rustling of trees in the breeze serenaded him into a doze.

"Does the angel have a name?"

Ra-el jolted out of his trance at the disruption. "Uh I...Ra-el. I'm Ra-el," he clarified. "Do...you have a name too?"

"Zero."

"Well, good night then Zero," he whispered.

Zero only grunted in reply.

*

Ra-el awoke to chaos. He felt something grab his upper arm and drag him across the ground. Madly blinking sleep from his eyes, he tried to make sense of what was happening. A Nephilim had his arm firmly grasped, and another grabbed his second arm.

"Look who's awake."

He identified the speaker as Morag, one of his town's top guards. "L-let go of me."

"Not a chance in heaven. Order Falsyn made it pretty clear that you're to come back and receive your punishment, dirt-groveler." Morag's expression was smug.

Anger burned inside Ra-el, but he couldn't do much more than squirm.

"If you don't let me go right now, a demonoid dragon will come and—"

Morag threw back his head and laughed heartily. "The purple one? He's not gonna do a thing." He gestured to the cave's entrance.

Ra-el's heart sank. Zero was standing there, Nephilim by his side. A large sack sat at the dragon's feet, filled with what looked like gems and money. His hiding place had been

sold for material riches. It felt like a punch to the gut.
"How could you…?" he began, staring at Zero, crushed.

Zero shrugged with a smirk.
"Never trust a demon," was his reply. He grabbed the sack
and spread his wings, taking off into the morning air.

"Are you seriously surprised to be betrayed by a
demon? Ha," Morag chuckled, shaking his head. "Idiot," he
added quietly.

Before Ra-el could gather his thoughts, something
hard struck the back of his head and he passed out.
*

Ra-el opened his eyes groggily, trying to figure out
where he was. The cave? No, the ground was too smooth.
There were patterns in the stone, patterns he knew all too
well.

"Quite the adventure you had."

That was Order Falsyn's voice, he was sure of it. He
groaned and rose to a slumped sitting position. A pounding
headache assaulted his brain and a wave of nausea rose from
his core. He shut his eyes tightly, listening to his booming
heartbeat, until the sickness passed.

"Any final words as a Nephilim? No, never mind, you
don't deserve any," Order Falsyn sneered.

It was hard to say how he felt. Despair? Anger? A
bitter sadness? Empty, that was it; he simply felt empty. He
had dissociated with everything going on around him. It was
someone else he was watching. Someone else's end. There
was a strange tranquility to it all. He sagged down further, his
forehead nearly touching the ground.

He could hear Order Falsyn approaching. It was
just like the day before, except this time, there would be
no escape. He didn't have the strength to fly, nor the will.
He'd lost. Been sold out by someone he thought might be
an ally. And for what? A small amount of treasure? His fist
curled against the stone floor. He was a fool for believing the

dragon would ever help him.

"Have fun rotting in Hell, miscreant." Order Falsyn touched his shoulder.

The sound of shattering glass disrupted the scene. Something hefty landed hard on the ground, crunching more glass beneath it. Order Falsyn whipped his head around to face the intruder and was promptly shoved into a wall. A mad cackle echoed in the chamber.

"What do you think you're doing? You already got your payment, so get out of here." Order Falsyn squirmed out of his attacker's grasp, making for the door.

"Ha! Never trust a demon." Zero grinned mischievously, a glint in his eyes. He tucked his wings in and pounced again, scratching at an indignant Falsyn. He swung his tail around and knocked the Order member to the ground, then pinned him down with a clawed foot.

Order Falsyn, realizing the beast wasn't going to back down, whispered something inaudible and a luminous white blade appeared in his hand. Its hilt was indistinguishable from the blade, carved from one shimmering chunk of angelic ore. He stabbed at his assailant's shoulder, barely piercing such a thick hide.

Zero snorted, pleased at Falsyn's futile efforts. He grabbed the Order's blade wrist and pinned it to the ground. "That the best you got?" he snarked.

"Guards!" Order Falsyn yelled, glaring daggers at Zero.

Ra-el, his head still pounding, mustered the last of his strength for one last shot at freedom. He knew dozens of Order members would soon be upon them, and despite Zero's sheer size and muscle, there was no way the two of them would get out alive.

"We have to go!" he shouted hoarsely, his eyes darting between the door and Zero.

Zero was not impressed. He grunted and rolled his

eyes. Without a word he picked Order Falsyn up and flung him into the nearest pillar, winding him to buy them time. "Fine," he answered, running across the room to Ra-el. With a massive clawed hand he grabbed the weakened Nephilim and slung him over his shoulder.

Zero ran to the shattered window and flew out just as the main door burst open and several Nephilim flooded the room. He could see their hesitation between helping the injured Order or pursuing him. With a few strong wingbeats, he sailed through town and past the meadows of spring flowers. He ripped a few out in passing, flinging them into the breeze with a laugh. No one followed him. He dipped over the edge of the floating landmass and disappeared into the clouds, Ra-el clinging to his back.

*

"Why help me?" Ra-el was sitting on the cave floor—a different one—leaning against the cool wall. He sipped the herbal tea he had bought from the nearby town, letting the warmth and aroma soothe his fading headache. "I mean, you got paid. Why bother coming back for me?"

Zero was face deep in an animal carcass, snapping muscles and bones like twigs. He raised his head, now painted crimson, to look at Ra-el.
"Easy. You owe me now, angel." He ripped another piece of meat off, throwing his head back to swallow it in one gulp. "I can keep razing villages, you heal me when I get hurt, it's perfect."

Ra-el sighed and shook his head. He did owe the demon, that was true. While he wasn't keen on the idea of watching the dragon terrorize innocent villagers, he reminded himself their agreement could work to his benefit. Zero wanted him around, after all, which meant he had the protection of the demonoid. He could travel the world and help common folk like he dreamed of. Plus, he figured he could maybe change Zero's mind about all the chaos and destruction. Maybe.

"Guess I don't have a choice," Ra-el smiled and took another sip of tea.

He didn't know what the future would bring, but as long as he could use his powers to help people, he would be happy. He looked out from the cave across meadows of blooming wildflowers and budding trees, and felt a deep peace settle into his bones. Whatever happened, he knew it would be new and exciting.

How a Dragon Saved a Kingdom
Rosalyn Maris Franics

Once upon a time in a far away kingdom there lived a king who lived with his wife, the Queen, three sons, and three daughters. Everyday after his sons' lessons with the tutors, their father, King Victor, questioned them about what they learnt. This always took place in the royal court with courtiers looking upon the spectacle.

Gregor the eldest son's face burned with shame when his father frowned at his answers, for he always made a serious attempt to give good answers. His tutor persisted in telling him that if his younger brothers showed themselves more intelligent than he would lose his place as first in line for the throne. Gregor feared ending up a pitiful, wandering knight with no home, fighting for food and board at the behest of any lord who would hire him. He worked hard at coming up with the very best answers he could, his brothers' foolishness and prattle would get smiles or even laughs from the courtiers leaving Gregor feeling aggrieved. Gregor was not a happy, young man.

Gregor's brothers, David and Randolph, would often leave things in Gregor's pockets especially as they left the classroom so he no longer dared to touch his clothing for fear a frog or snake would land on the stone floor of the audience hall. Lady Pauline often accused him to trying to send all the ladies of the court into fainting fits. This embarrassed Gregor even more and sometimes he hated his brothers.

Once he'd had answered questions in court, Gregor spend time learning to use weapons and hone battle strategy from the head of the King's army, a no non-sense man. Gregor could not win there either. He was made to fight with

13

whichever of the king's guard were on hand. These men were twice as large as Gregor and he often ended up with bruising that would linger long past the next lesson, so he was always sore.

The only person who sympathized was Lord Donald, a distant cousin of the Queen, but the King never asked for his advice. The Queen listened but never acted on his advice. Donald listened to the young prince's woes. Gregor learned that Lord Donald would listen at the age of five when his brother, David, had broken his hobby horse and his parents had told him that a toy was not important enough reason to beat this brother.

Now Donald would wait for the young prince in the hall as he come back from his battle lessons and bemoan Gregor's bruises and his poor showing in court. Lord Donald criticized the King's decisions to Gregor, expressing dismay at things like inviting people from the nations around them to dine at the expense of the kingdom. It was ridiculous to pay full price for the goods his vassals produced and his traders imported, rather than taxing their goods from them.

Gregor sometimes wanted to argue with Donald but then who would listen to his woes. Rather than cause dissention, Gregor instead ask Donald how he would rule the kingdom if he was king. Donald would look pleased and go about what would happen if he would king. Gregor found that listening helped to understand why his tutors taught what they did.

Once supper was over, the princes would get their daily hour with their mother, the Queen. She would send her ladies-in-waiting away and talk to her sons and daughters. This was only time Gregor got to see his sisters, whose governesses taught female virtues and housekeeping in other parts of the castle.

"Mother, can you tell us a story?" Gregor's eldest sister Catherine asked. "We are filled up to the eyebrows with nonsensical lessons about not walking outside on the first day of spring."

The Queen frowned. "It is not nonsense. The rule about the first day of spring has a sad history that we must not ignore and if you do not know the why of it then that is the story I shall tell. Many years ago, when this land was still forest it was home to a dragon, a very ferocious animal with teeth six-feet long and breath so horrid it would kill you just to smell it.

"The first king of this land needed a new home when the last one had been overrun with barbarians. He and his court arrived in summer and for almost a whole year they heard and saw nothing of this dragon. No one lived here to tell them about it. All through the winter they lived in shabby buildings for they had not had time to build anything better and ate boiled turnips and raw cabbage for lack of anything better. The king at the urging of the court planned to celebrate the coming of the first day of spring when they would start to eat the new plants. Everyone was so looking forward to this spring event.

"The servants went out to gather the wild plants early in the morning, but something seemed different, but no one could put their finger on the reason. As people woke up, they went outside to enjoy the first sunny day of the year. An hour before the planned feast one of the servants came running into the building saying yelling something. The king had to calm the man, but eventually he said that this large bird with long teeth had come down and eaten all the servants it could snatch. It swallowed them whole and ate everything else in sight.

"The king ordered his knights to kill it, but the creature was covered in hard shells and their spears and swords only bounced off. It ate half the knights who tried to kill it and the others were forced to run for their lives. It was a disaster for the kingdom, and it took many years for the kingdom to groom more knights and many servants had to do two jobs until the next generation could be trained."

"Did the king kill the dragon, Mom?" One of the little sisters who hugged tight to Gregor's side asked.

"No, no one knew how, and the surprising thing was that it was not until the next year, the first sunny day of spring that the beast reappeared. Only this time the king ordered his warriors to watch for the beast and note the damage. The beast again woke up, but it went after the deer and other animals since the people stayed protected in the buildings which had been much upgraded over the previous year. The king decreed that no one should go out the next spring but that a large amount of cattle should be left where the dragon could see them, so it would eat and go back to sleep."

Gregor saw from his face that Randolph was interested in the story and he worried briefly about what that meant but he knew that his brothers would be watched closely on the first day of spring, the brothers always had been. The sisters seemed scared which to Gregor was a reasonable response.

"The King will keep us safe." Gregor told to his sisters. "No one will force you outside on the first day of spring."

His mother smiled at him. "Gregor is right, we have lived here many generations now and so long as we feed the dragon on the first day of spring, no one will come to harm."

One day when Gregor was especially sore, he stopped to rest in a small area off the main corridor. He leaned against the wall and heard Lord Donald's voice.

"The nobility is being forced to pay the tradesmen and traders far too much money because the king refuses to pay less than full price. They rob us and then King Victor demands that we, instead of they, pay taxes."

"You are right, Lord Donald, but how do we change

it? You have the young prince's ear."

"The prince is taught to follow his father, he will not change it," Lord Donald sneered. "He is a weakling. You hear the foolish things he says in court."

Gregor listened carefully at the voice of the other for it sounds like his father's chief advisor.
"What do you think we should do?" Is the man's answer to Lord Donald. Gregor heard Donald's answer get frightened then angry.

Gregor thinks about it and goes to his meeting with Lord Donald. He has to hide his anger. Instead he says.
"How long the winter is stretching out. I will be relieved when the second day of spring comes, and we spend time outside. This castle is so gloomy in winter."

"The second day of spring?" Donald frowned. "Why wait?"

"The King forbids us to enjoy the first sunny day of spring," Gregor answered. "It is regarded as a holiday for the servants before the year's work begins."

Lord Donald frowned. "For what reason?"

Gregor paused. "The tutors have not said and neither has my father." Gregor refused to say more about it before he bids Lord Donald good night although Donald pressed him for answers.

One day David came to Gregor, "Randolph and I wish to see the dragon."

"Then on the first day of spring sneak up the guard's tower and leave the trap door open. Once you have seen the dragon jump back down the hole before it sees you," Gregor told him.

"Have you ever seen the dragon? Maybe we should kill it?" His brother frowned.

"You are better than the king's knights that you can slay a dragon?" Gregor shook his head. "Leave it a year, this year the dragon is helping me with a problem."

David frowned at his elder brother but said nothing more.

As the weeks past, Lord Donald came around less and less, but Gregor eavesdropped on his conversations with others and gathered a list of people who talked to Lord Donald and agreed with him. When Lord Donald did come, Gregor made sure to mention the first day of spring and the fact that all work came to a halt. Soon mention of the wasted day sent Lord Donald into a rant.

His brothers come progressively later and later to the tutoring room, Gregor got his brothers alone. "The tutors will go to father soon if you come any later."

"We are trying to find the dragon while he still sleeps," Randolph told him.

"It is not with an hour's walk of the castle and we dare not go further for fear of not being in the tutor room before time. Father would send a search party if we were not to show," David answered. "Perhaps you can convince him to let us explore further."

Gregor shook his head. "I doubt he would let me. I told you if you want to see the dragon without being eaten the guard tower on the first day of spring would be the best place to see it."

"How do we get away from the guards?" David asked.

"That you would have to figure out that day. It will depend upon the circumstances," Gregor answered. "What are you going to do when you see it? Why do you want to see it?"

Randolph smiled. "I want draw a picture of it."

Gregor laughs. "Then you'd better take an easel with you." They go off to the tutor room for their lesson.

A week before the first day of spring, Lord Donald waited for him after his fighting lesson. Gregor is tired. Lord Donald talked about the many mistakes the King was making in negotiating with a nearby lord instead of taking his mine by force. The rates the lord wanted for his coal were outrageous Lord Donald insisted.

Gregor shrugged. "It is my father's privilege to have it so. He is King."

Lord Donald started. "If I were king..."

"But you are not and have no right to an option other than the one you are given," Gregor answered. "Your advice is neither needed or wanted. My mother may humour you but no one else cares."

Lord Donald reddened. "I have friends who listen."

"None of them would step out the door with you the first day of spring in rebellion to the king," Gregor answered. "Your rebellion will come to nothing."

"They will follow me." Lord Donald argued but walked away at the sound of footsteps. Gregor watched him go with remorse for the lost friendship, but he did not call him back. The servants would tell him no and when he had to go alone Lord Donald would crumble.

Gregor eavesdropped on the servants for the next week and what little he hears suggested that the servants were not ready to step outside on the first day of spring. He felt relief that he judged right. The day before spring's arrival when he and his brothers come for their daily questioning Lord Donald stands before the king demanding that people be allowed to work outside on the day of spring.

King Victor frowned. "It is for our safety that we remain inside tomorrow. We will keep the tradition of this country."

"Safety, it is ridiculous to believe it would be less safe to go outside tomorrow than today," Lord Donald proclaims. "The treasury loses a day's profit for nothing."

King Victor frowns. "It is the law of the land."

"The law needs to be changed!" Lord Donald frowns. The court whispers as Lord Donald takes his stand. "Anyone should be able to walk freely out of the castle tomorrow."

"Let him, sire, walk out the door for he incites your servants to rebellion," Gregor answered.

King Victor glanced at his sons. David spoke up. "I have heard people talking and their speech is treasonous."

"Lord Donald will walk out the door and anyone who wishes may go with him," King Victor decrees.

The next morning, Lord Donald stands among a few courtiers and household servants when Gregor and his brothers peeked around the corner from door standing next to the door of the guard's tower.

"I believed none would leave with him," Gregor commented and steps closer. He blocks the view to the tower door next to him and allows his brothers access.

"I have given my word that they can leave, open the door," King Victor orders and the guard opens the door.

"It is a beautiful day," Lord Donald commented as he walked out. At the last moment four of the kitchen maids stop walking a dozen paces from the door. They hurry towards the kitchen.

King Victor watched until the group until they step out of sight and the guard closed the door.
"Open it if they knock," King Victor tells the guards. The men nod. A great wind shrieks outside the building and a sudden squeal comes from the guard tower before David and Randolph appear at the door and slam it shut with their backs to it.

King Victor came over to where his sons tremble. Gregor considers his punishment for helping them.
"Where were you?" the King demands.

"We went up and peeked out to see the dragon." David fought for the breath to speak.
"What can you tell us about the dragon?" Gregor asks.

"It is the mountain top," Randolph said.
King Victor frowns. "Enough of your pranks. The mountain top is rock."

"No, father, Randolph is telling the truth. The dragon lifted its head and the top came off the mountain. When it flew the rest of the rock lifted from the mountain. The dragon sleeps on the top of a large hill and it is the mountain top," David answered. "It can hunt it successfully now."

"You shall not hunt it at all," Gregor said. "For it saved us from Lord Donald and his rebellion. We owe the dragon our gratitude."

King Victor frowns. "Did the dragon see Lord Donald and his followers?"

"We did not stay long enough to see where it went," David answered, "Once it was in the air and flying, we came back down the trap door. Gregor warned us about allowing him to see us."

Randolph nods. "We did not want to be eaten."

"I had not thought about observing the dragon from the tower. Perhaps we should check to see if any of Lord Donald's group will return. The dragon might have seen the cattle first and not eaten the people." King Victor places his hand on Gregor's shoulder. "Come, you will see just what destruction your plotting has wrought."

Gregor climbed the stairs under his father's grip. They see the dragon off in the distance where the cattle waited. Lord Donald's cloak laid ripped and torn on the ground. A servant crawled towards the door missing part of one leg.

"My son, those people have families and others who will miss them," King Victor scolded.

"But they were ready to make Lord Donald king and kill our family." Gregor frowns. "Is it not my duty to protect my brothers and sisters, my mother, and you from harm? Is that not what you are having the tutor teach me? To protect my land from war for economic and political reasons."

"It is my son, you are right," King Victor answers. "I

have forgotten because I dislike killing."

"You did not kill, father, you let them decide their own fate," Gregor answered. "You gave them the freedom they requested."

Spring Fair
Tracey Bentley

"There you go, Spike" said Suvy as she handed her baby brother his big lemon balloon.

"Why is it yellow? Suvy, I'm a boy."

"It's the biggest size, Spike, for your special message." Spike took the time to read his ballroom.

MY BROTHER SPIKE IS A FIRECRACKER.

Spike beamed with pride and blew a little smoke heart for his sister. They were at the Dragon Spring Country Fair celebrating Spike's first year at The Imperial School of Prehistoric Dragons. As the current holder of the Dragon Challenge Cup, Suvy, or Vesuvius to give her full name, was guest of honour to open the fair and judge the competitions. They had two competitions at the Spring fair: one for Dragon abilities and one for Spring flowers and baking. Suvy had chosen Spike to accompany her as his reward for his school grades. The Spring fair was Spike's favourite because after the judging they could buy all the boilberry pies and lavafruit jam. His Mum loved jam and Dad adored pie. Spike had saved his pocket money so he could bring treats home for everyone even Fergus and Fantail, the terrible twins.

As they walked around the fair, the smells of all the lovely food filled the air. Suvy bought Spike a huge sweet cake in the shape of a Princess! Yes, it was a pink princess, but this time Spike didn't mind the girly colour. It was easily double the size of his small paws but that didn't stop him from eating it all up. He had crumbs all round his snout so Suvy wiped them off with her handkerchief. Spike squirmed a little as he always did at clean up time, but it was a small sacrifice after such a lovely, huge treat.

An older female Dragon approached Suvy and Spike as they watched the George and Dragon show.

"Excuse me, Miss Scorchius, my name is Suki. I am your guide for the day. It's time for you to judge the flower competition," the older Dragon said.

Spike hadn't seen this type of Dragon before but judging by her accent she was definitely oriental. She appeared black at first but when the sun shone on her scales they were the deepest blue.

"What type of Dragon is she?" whispered Spike to Suvy as they followed behind.

"She is a Cantonese Midnight Dragon," replied Suvy. "A very rare and old breed".

Spike and Suvy made their way to the tent where the flowers were. It had a long name starting with H and he thought he would ask Suvy how to say the word when she had finished judging. The colours were incredible and Spike lost count of the different types of flower. Suki explained the competition was open to both Dragon world and human world flowers so there would be separate competitions for each. Collecting flowers and seeds from the human world was dangerous and took a lot of skill, especially with big paws and claws! Spike thought these Dragons were the coolest in the world, so he was shocked to see all the competitors were older female Dragons.

Suvy walked round looking at all the different blooms, occasionally taking the time to smell the beautiful scent. She asked the competitors questions and listened carefully to the answers. A couple of the ladies gave Spike a smile or some candies, boy he loved the fuss and this V.I.P. lifestyle. Suvy handled herself with poise and grace, always showing an interest in her champion duties and making the competitors feel special. Suvy chose her winner for human flowers, a Dragon called Ethel with a beautiful Camelia flower. She gave her a rosette and certificate which Ethel held high for all to see.

On to Dragon world plants now! The colours were just as beautiful but there was a lot more reds and oranges. Spike was still amazed at how many flowers grew in the Dragon world. Maybe he would tell GranDragon Scorchius when he saw her at holiday time, she loved flowers too. Suvy looked at so many competitors, how could she choose? After lots of comparing, measuring and smelling she decided on an Embergladia, a rich orange flower that was a perfect match to the last glow from a bonfire. The winner this time was a Welsh Red called Margaret. She pinned her rosette on her gardener's vest and was very proud.

Suvy and Spike had a little break then they headed to the jam tent. Suvy had scorched some autographs for young Dragons as they walked around and some of them even asked Spike for his scorch mark. This little Dragon was having the best day ever, and now there was lots of jam! There was the usual lavafruit then there was boilberry, flameapple, hotmelon and scalplum! Suvy tasted each jam on a little cracker and narrowed the competition down to two scalplums and a boilberry. Spike got to taste just the finalist's jam as Suvy didn't want to make her little brother sick with lots of sugar.

After much deliberation and recipe checking the winner was the scalplum by Nora, a feisty old water Dragon. She gave Spike a whole jar to himself! He could just about wrap his paws round it but he held on tight. Suvy had to judge the pies next. Spike didn't go with her this time. He had a tummy ache from all the jam tasting so he sat quietly in the V.I.P tent. After Suvy had finished judging, she came back for Spike and they both returned to the food tent to buy pies and jam for the rest of the family.

As Suvy and Spike were heading for the V.I.P. tent with the treats for the family Suki caught up with them.

"It's time for you to judge the tower climb, please,

Suvy," she said.

"Okay," replied Suvy "Lead the way!" Spike was so excited, this was the Dragon contest he had been waiting for. The trio went to the back of the field where a large tower had been erected for the contest.

Twelve large teenage Dragons were warming up, stretching their limbs, checking their claws and unfolding their wings. Flying was not allowed during the climb but they would need wing balance nearer the top.

Suki the Cantonese Dragon flapped her wings and blew out a bright flame to signal they were ready to start. Spike couldn't help admiring how big her wingspan was for such a petite Dragon. He was fascinated at how she could fold them up so small!

"Attention, please competitors." The field fell silent. For a female Dragon, Suki had a booming voice.

"Please welcome, Vesuvius the Great and Powerful, current holder of the Challenge Cup."

The crowd and competitors flapped their wings as Suvy stood and gave a slight bow. She blew a bright orange flame in acknowledgement of their applause.

The first competitor got to the start line at the base of the tower. It rose about ninety feet in the air and they had to climb up, light the flame then return and ring the bell.

The whistle blew and the first Dragon was off! He was a Peruvian Serpent Face and very agile. This particular Dragon breed was known to be quick and this young man didn't disappoint. He scaled the tower easily with his strong claws, only needing a brief wing balance as he lit the flame at the top. Within thirty seconds, the Serpent Face was back down and ringing the bell with his tail.

Spike was in awe of this athletic feat. Even though they had towers at his school they hadn't been climbed in quite a while. Suvy flapped politely then put a scorch mark on his result sheet. The climb wasn't just about speed, his technique would play a big part in the competition. A Rubbletail flew to the top of the tower to extinguish the flame ready for the next competitor.

"How quick are you, Suvy?" whispered Spike.

"Fourteen seconds, little bro," she replied.

Spike stared open mouthed at his big sister and hoped that one day he could follow in her pawsteps and be that awesome!!

The second competitor took their position. Spike had never seen such a beautiful coloured Dragon in his life. He tried to find the dominant shade but he just couldn't.

"Please welcome, Shenyah, all the way from Barbados. Shenyah is a Caribbean Rainbow Scale and is the first of her breed to compete in any Dragon competitions." Shenyah acknowledged the crowd with a wing stretch. Spike could certainly see where this type of Dragon got its name as she revealed so many colours in her underwing. The whistle blew and she started her climb. Spike could tell she had a lot more control than the last Dragon but not quite as quick. It would be very interesting to see the outcome.

One by one the competitors took on the challenge of the climb and Spike was fascinated by every single one. He began to understand how both speed and technique mattered in this particular discipline. He made a mental note to ask Suvy about climb training in the summer. Yes, he was only in his first year at school but you can never start these things too young.

Competitor number seven, another Peruvian Serpent Face ripped a claw part way up the tower and had to retire from the competition. As the first aid attendant rushed to the aid of the injured Dragon Spike recognised her as the nurse from his school. He waved a paw.

"Nurse Reddy, it's me Spike," Spike called out, getting up from his chair as he waved.

The nurse was very busy with her patient but still

looked at Spike and blew a little smoke, "Hello."

He sat back down and was quite pleased with himself. Spike was recognised.

The last Dragon completed the challenge and after some deliberations and calculations the winner was announced.

"The best technical climb today goes to Shenyah." Everyone flapped their congratulations as the Rainbow Scale stood to acknowledge the crowd.

"The Kiwi Thrashtail has taken twenty-two seconds and our Judge Vesuvius was very impressed with his technique and balance," announced Suki.

"Please welcome, Horace to the winners stand."

A big pale blue Dragon rushed to the stage flapping his wings and almost taking off in his excitement. Spike could see a group of similar Dragons in the crowd and he assumed they were Horace's proud family.

Suvy presented Horace with a banner and a little tower trophy. He blushed as she shook his paw but eventually found his voice and asked for an autograph. Suvy scorched the side of the banner with a V taking care not to hurt Horace in the process. He smiled widely as he left the stage. Suki cleared her throat ready for the next announcement.

"In ten minutes, the baby breathers' event will be starting. The competition is open to all Dragons seven years old and under."

Spikes eyes lit up, a fire breathing competition.

"Can I join in, Suvy? Can I pleeaasee?" he pleaded with his older sister.

"I need to check I'm not judging it, Spike," replied Suvy as she turned and went to see Suki.

"Suki," called Suvy as she got closer to the stage. "Am I required to judge the baby breathers or can my young brother join in?".

"Of course, he can join in," said Suki with a smile.

"It's just a timed event with no technical input or style required."

When Suvy told Spike he could join in, he flapped so hard he almost flew off.

The couple made their way to the arena for the competition and they were surprised to see so many entries. Spike swallowed hard and felt nervous. He didn't see any of his classmates, but he recognised some of the older Dragons from school. At five years old, he was one of the youngest competitors. Spike gave his name nervously to the Welsh Red Dragon taking the entries.

"Spike Scorchius," he said quietly. The Red looked up and saw Suvy stood behind Spike. If she didn't recognise Spike's last name, she certainly recognised his sister.

The object of the competition was to burn a small wooden stake in the fastest time possible. There were twenty-five stakes in the ground awaiting the competitors. Suki had made her way to the arena and was ready to announce the start.

"Due to the large number of entrants this year, we will have some elimination rounds before the grand final. The first twenty competitors to burn their stake will carry on in the competition. All Dragons will receive a certificate for taking part today." A murmur of agreement was heard from the adult Dragons as the children flapped with excitement.

Spike took his place.

"3.2.1. GO."

He blew so hard the flame was bright red in a second. He had burnt his stake to the ground in just over fifteen seconds and was eighth fastest. He was into the next round! Suvy hugged her little brother so tight he could hardly breathe.

"I said you were a firecracker when we first got here," she said pointing to his lemon balloon she was now holding. Spike blushed. He was in ecstasy, not only had he made the next round he had been quicker than over half of the rest of the other Dragons. Two of those eliminated were Nevada Hotheads, the Cactus twins from year three at school. Hotheads were renowned for their abilities in fire breathing but not today! Those eliminated went to collect their certificates.

As the stakes were set up for round two, Suvy showed Spike some lung and nostril exercises to improve his performance.

"Time to up your game, little bro," she said as she massaged his ears, the Scorchius secret weapon was the ear wiggle.

Spike stood at his stake
"3.2.1. GO."

Ears wiggled and Spike blew as hard as he could. Fourteen seconds this time still got Spike to the next round, but he noticed most of the other Dragons were faster too. The old Siberian Grey Cloud who was setting up the stakes stopped and sniffed the air. Suvy looked up and saw dark storm clouds gathering. Grey Cloud Dragons were very aware of changes in weather conditions and the old Siberian was talking urgently with Suki. She quickly announced the next round and Spike took his position. This time he was even more determined.

Eleven seconds and seventh fastest! Spike was on a roll. He felt wonderful and so proud of his achievements. The fact that Suvy was watching made this event even more special.

As the Siberian Grey put in the second stake, he looked up and sniffed, dropped the other stakes and ran from the arena.

CRACK!

The clap of thunder was so loud it shook Spike from the tip of his snout to the last scale on his tail. The lightning that followed was neon blue and it split the sky in half, letting the contents of the storm clouds plummet to the ground. As everyone ran for cover, Spike just watched mesmerised. He'd never realised how beautiful an electrical storm could be. Suvy scooped up her little brother and ran to the VIP area with Suki. The lightning intensified, flashing blues and purples into the sky like fireworks. The occasional bright white flash lit up the sky shedding light on the many fleeing Dragon families that had abandoned the fair.

"You must go," shouted Suki trying to be heard over the thunder. "This type of storm can last for hours in these parts."

"Ok," replied Suvy. "Thank you for your hospitality."

She quickly shook Suki's paw before collecting the jam and pies, lifting Spike on to her back as she opened her wings and took off. The little Dragon hung on to his big sister with all his might. He knew Suvy was a safe flyer, but this storm was fierce and very scary. Spike still couldn't help admiring all the colours of the lightning. As it forked again and again, he imagined the sky as a shattered mirror, each shard being a different pattern to the other.

Suvy was very quick on the wing, swooping occasionally to avoid other families fleeing to the safety of their caves. The thunder was still so loud a couple of cracks even made her jump. Spike was finished admiring the storm, he just kept his eyes closed. Suvy was at full speed now and, boy, was she fast.

As the pair arrived home, Spike could see his mum and dad waiting for them anxiously at the mouth of their cave. Although the storm was raging at home, it lacked the intensity he'd seen at the fair.

"We were so worried," said mum as she hugged Suvy then Spike.

"Just a little," said dad, "but I knew Vesuvius the Great and Powerful would make sure everyone got home safely." Fergus and Fantail came running out of the cave and rubbed Spike's ears.

"Boys, I entered the baby breathers competition! I got through three rounds before the storm came."

"Well done, Spikey boy, that's our baby brother," said Fergus.

"You'll win next year, I'm sure," added Fantail.

"We brought pies and jam for everybody. It's all super nice," said Spike

"Come on, children, everyone inside for supper," said mum as she started back into the cave.

"Won't be a minute, Mum," shouted Spike as everyone else went inside.

The little green North Atlantic Emeraldback Dragon sat at the mouth of the cave staring up at the vivid colours of the storm. He dreamed of next year's country fair and winning baby breathers.

Oh yes, get ready people, Spike Scorchius is one determined little Dragon!

Gerald the Dragon
B. Heather Mantler

Gerald wasn't an old dragon, but his eyesight was not the same as when he was young. He disputed that fact whenever it was brought to his attention and claimed to see fine. Most definitely it got worse every year.

His eyesight was the last thing on Gerald's mind as he crawled out of his cave after sleeping through a long winter. He turned his head towards the sun and stretched his wings to their full span. It felt good to move. It would feel better once he found some food.

Gerald finished his stretching before taking to the air. If he remembered correctly there was a field of sheep close by. It took only a moment for Gerald to spot the field of white animals. He carefully picked one out and started into his dive.

His talons closed around the sheep and Gerald headed for the top of the nearest hill. He landed and looked down at what was supposed to be his meal. Rather than a sheep, the creature in his talons was a pure white unicorn. And the unicorn was glaring at him.

"Do you mind?" the voice was gruff.

"Sorry," Gerald said as he opened his talons so the unicorn could walk free. The unicorn started to trot away. Then he stopped and tossed one comment over his shoulder before leaving.

"Get your eyes checked."

Gerald stared at where the unicorn had gone. Do they make glasses big enough for dragons?

About the Authors

JENNIE EVANS is a Kelowna-born writer and artist. When she's not drawing weird and wonderful fantasy creatures, she can be found passionately ranting about wildlife and plants to anyone who will listen. Her favourite animals are crows and ravens.

ROSALYN MARIE FRANICS is a wife and mother of three and a grandmother of one. She lives in Penticton, BC and writes novels. She is a avid reader of a wide variety of things and dreams of having a garden again so she can get her hands dirty.

TRACEY BENTLEY is 49-years-old and originally come from Salford, just outside Manchester, England. After successful careers in international banking and ballroom dancing, she has returned to her childhood passion, storytelling. She is honing her passion by studying creative writing at Okanagan College and living in "Beautiful British Columbia" with her partner and two greyhounds.

B. HEATHER MANTLER is a lover of fairy tales and fables. Her home town is Prince George, British Columbia. Heather is always working on another story as she hopes to finish every story idea that she has ever written down. Her blog is heathersdomain.wordpress.com.